This edition published by Parragon Books Ltd in 2015

Parragon Books Ltd
Chartist House
15–17 Trim Street
Bath BA1 1HA, UK
www.parragon.com

ISBN 978-1-4723-   -8

Printed in China

COLLECTION

Contents

PaRRagon

Tangled
Ever After

Illustrated by Studio IBOIX

$\mathcal{S}$pring had sprung and Flynn had a surprise for Rapunzel. They took a walk through the forest.

Flynn wanted to be alone with Rapunzel, but Maximus wanted to keep guard and Pascal went along to play.

Finally, evening came and Flynn took his chance to jump into a boat with Rapunzel. The lovely night reminded them of when they had first watched the floating lanterns together.

Flynn put his hand in his pocket – he was going to propose! But, oops, he did need Pascal and Max after all, because they had the ring!

"Will you marry me?" Flynn finally asked.
"Yes!" Rapunzel replied happily.

On their way home Rapunzel
wanted to tell everyone their news!

The thugs from The Snuggly Duckling were delighted.
It turned out they had always wanted a wedding to plan!
They each had their own ideas about the special day.

One of them helped Rapunzel to design a cake.

They baked and iced, but
nothing seemed quite right.
But, finally, they
created the wedding cake of
Rapunzel's dreams!

Next, Tor helped Rapunzel
choose the flowers.

Rapunzel's favourites were
the wild flowers picked
from a nearby field.

As for who would carry the rings –
the choice was easy! Maximus and Pascal
were very proud to accept.

When it was time to find a wedding dress Rapunzel wanted to design her own. She drew lots of pictures … but simply could not make up her mind!

The pub thugs tried to help, but their dresses didn't seem right either.

Luckily, the Queen arrived. "Darling," she said, "I want to help you find the perfect dress."

And she did….

On the morning of the wedding, bells rang throughout the kingdom. Everyone was excited to see the King and Queen riding happily in the royal coach.

Max and Pascal were excited too – that is, until Max sneezed and the rings flew into the air!

As Max and Pascal chased after the rings, the King proudly offered his arm to Rapunzel to walk up the aisle.

Flynn was so happy when he saw
Rapunzel in her beautiful dress.
Luckily, nobody had any idea
what Max and Pascal were up to....

They were racing through the kingdom after the rings!
Max and Pascal were causing a lot of chaos.

Max ran straight through some
drying clothes as he chased one ring …

… and Pascal
chased the other ring
into the air.

They finally caught the runaway rings ... but then they crashed right into the tar factory!

Max and Pascal quickly left the factory and raced to the wedding. They arrived just in time!

Even though their ring-bearers now looked a bit strange, Flynn and Rapunzel were glad they were there.

Flynn and Rapunzel's friends helped
to make the reception perfect.
The couple danced their first dance.

They cut the wedding cake
and were the first to taste it.
It was delicious!

And as the newly married couple
rode away in their wedding coach
Rapunzel cried out happily …

"Best. Day. Ever!"

Snow White
and the
Great Jewel Hunt

By Kitty Richards
Illustrations by The Disney Storybook Artists

"*Farewell*, my love!" said Snow White. The Prince was leaving on a royal trip. It was the first time the newlyweds would be apart.

"I'll be home soon," replied the Prince. "Until then, I've left an envelope for you on the well. It's the first clue in a treasure hunt. At the end, you'll find a special gift!"

"Why, a well is where we first met," Snow White told the Seven Dwarfs.

The clue was in plain sight.
The Dwarfs gathered around as
Snow White opened the envelope.

"I wonder what the gift will be?"
she said, then she read:

"*Can't leave you a kiss,
Or even a hug,
So here is a clue:
Look under the....*"

"I know!" cried Sneezy. "The Prince
left the next clue under a bug!"
Sleepy yawned. "Bug?" he asked.
"Are you sure?" said Snow White.
Sneezy nodded and led everyone to
the garden.

Snow White and the Dwarfs looked under ladybirds,
butterflies, beetles and, very carefully, bumblebees.
But they didn't find a thing.

"Actually, it would be pretty hard to hide a clue
under a bug," said Snow White. "Maybe it's hidden under
something that sounds like bug?"

"Under a jug?" suggested Happy.

"No, he must have meant under a mug!" said Grumpy.

Back inside, Grumpy announced, "To the kitchen!"
Then he nearly tripped over Dopey.

"Crawling on the floor in someone's castle is mad banners,"
scolded Doc. "I mean, it's bad manners!"

"Whatever are you doing, Dopey?" asked Snow White.

Dopey crawled out from under the carpet and held up an envelope. Snow White clapped her hands with excitement. "Under the rug! Oh, Dopey, you're a genius!"

Snow White read the clue:

"Hooray, you found it!
Easy when you try.
Now in the kitchen
Just lift up the...."

"Pie!" shouted all the Dwarfs at the same time.
Searching had given them quite an appetite!

First, Snow White served everyone a big piece of freshly baked fruit pie. Then, while they were eating, she read the next clue. It was hidden underneath the pie plate.

"Put on a smile,
It's no time to frown.
You'll find the next clue
In your royal...."

Snow White thought for a moment. "My royal gown?" she guessed.

In Snow White's dressing room, the Dwarfs searched through gown, after gown, after gown. But there was no clue to be found.

Ah-choo! "Now we'll never find Snow White's gift," said Sneezy.

Grumpy noticed Bashful standing in
the corner. "Why aren't you searching?"
Grumpy asked him.

"Why, he doesn't have to,"
Snow White said. "He's wearing my royal
crown. That must be where the clue is!"

Bashful took off the crown ...

… and inside was the clue!

"The gift is almost yours.
My, my, this game has flown!
There's one thing left to do:
Just look upon your…."

"Stone!" offered Sneezy.
"That's silly," said Grumpy.
"It must be bone!"

Then all of the Dwarfs shouted ideas.

"Cone!"

"Dome!"

"Trombone!"

As the Seven Dwarfs guessed,
Snow White realized someone was missing.
"Where's Sleepy?" she asked. They all set
off to look for him.

But he wasn't in the dining room.

Or in the kitchen.

Or in the Great Hall.

Sleepy was sound asleep on
Snow White's royal throne.

"That's the answer to the clue," she whispered.
"Just look upon your throne."
"So where's the gift?" Grumpy grumped.
"Right there," said Doc. "Look!"
Sitting at the very top of Snow White's throne
were two birds holding something that sparkled.
"This is so exciting!" said Happy.

To everyone's surprise, the birds
flew down and placed a delicate necklace
around Snow White's neck. The gift
was a stunning heart-shaped ruby on
a golden chain.

"Why, it's the colour of love," she said.
Doc saw that Snow White was
holding something else. "The birds left
a note!" he cried.

Snow White opened the envelope and read aloud:

"Yes, jewels are lovely,
But as this hunt ends,
Keep one thought in mind:
The best gifts are...."

"Odds and ends," said Sneezy.
"No, it's definitely chickens and hens," said Happy.

Grumpy couldn't believe his ears. "What's wrong with you fellas? The answer is friends!"

"You're right," said Snow White. "I love my new necklace, but the best part of today was the time we spent together. Friends are the greatest gift of all!"

Magical Activities

Complete these princess puzzles and activities,
then turn to page 100 for the answers.

"Magic Mirror on the wall, who is the fairest one of all?"
Draw yourself in the mirror.

Doc and Dopey are making a necklace for Snow White.
Can you colour it?

1 = RED   2 = YELLOW   3 = BLUE

51

1. TDIOIPTEIY _____
2. IBTASITIHTFIUL _____
3. STINEETZIY _____
4. TSLIETEPTIY _____
5. IHTAIIPTPIY _____
6. IGRTIUMTPIY _____
7. TDIITOTIICT _____

Look at this picture of Snow White and her forest friends.
Then answer the questions below.

1. How many birds? _____

2. How many butterflies? _____

3. How many rabbits? _____

4. How many squirrels? _____

5. How many turtles? _____

53

Help the Prince find the missing glass slipper. Circle the slipper that matches the one in the Prince's hand.

Draw a picture of yourself at the ball.

Prince Charming's Ball

Find the following words in the pumpkin carriage below.
(Hint: You will find the words going down and across.)

Cinderella
prince
slipper
Gus
midnight
mice
pumpkin
ball
stepmother
gown

a	s	t	d	p	r	s	e	m	g
r	m	u	d	r	i	t	s	i	n
t	p	r	i	n	c	e	l	d	r
s	p	u	m	t	r	p	i	n	s
g	u	s	a	s	s	i	p	i	l
o	m	i	c	e	r	o	p	g	a
w	p	b	a	l	l	t	e	h	i
n	k	r	s	t	m	h	r	t	e
c	i	n	d	e	r	e	l	l	a
r	n	m	p	d	u	r	p	r	w

Help Cinderella's friends finish the surprise! Colour the dress pink, the stars yellow and the hearts purple.

Can you match these sentences with the pictures they describe?
Write the number of each sentence in the
circle beside the correct picture.

3) Cinderella's friends help her get dressed.

2) The Fairy Godmother comforts Cinderella.

1) The shoe fits!

Help Prince Phillip save Princess Aurora.
Connect the dots to reveal his magic sword.

Help Prince Phillip find his way to the castle so he can awaken Princess Aurora with a kiss.

START

FINISH

What gifts do the fairies give to Princess Aurora when she is a baby? Use the code below to find out.

A	B	C	D	E	F	G	H	I	J	K	L	M	N	O	P	Q	R	S	T	U	V	W	X	Y	Z
1	2	3	4	5	6	7	8	9	10	11	12	13	14	15	16	17	18	19	20	21	22	23	24	25	26

Flora gives the gift of _____ .

2	5	1	21	20	25

Fauna gives the gift of _____ .

19	15	14	7

Number these pictures in the order they happened.

Connect the dots to see Briar Rose's dance partner.

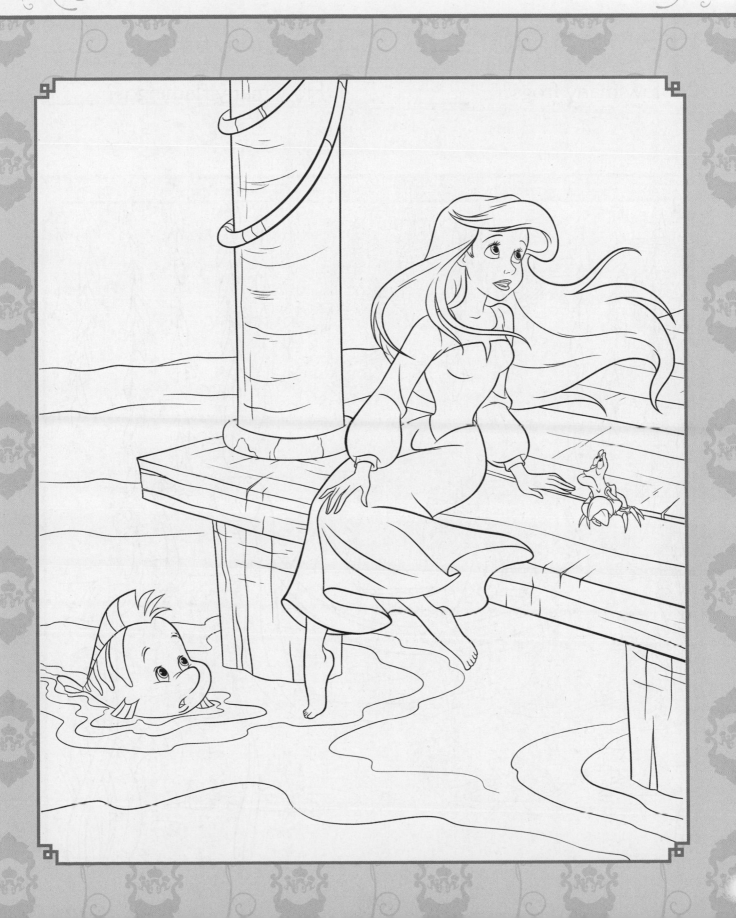

Look at this picture of Ariel, Eric and their animal friends.
Then answer the questions below.

1. How many seagulls? _____   3. How many fish? _____

2. How many frogs? _____   4. How many flamingos? _____

Join Ariel as she explores the shipwreck!
Look for the names listed on the right in the puzzle below.
(Hint: You will find them going down and across.)

```
k r s e a d t c g m p
i e p a z u l l r a r
n o u r s u l a r f i
g d n i u o s s y l n
t e r e p a c r w o c
r l a l d n u o d u e
i s e b a s t i a n e
t d p r e g t s e d r
o r m a x p l t n e i
n i n c s s e d w r c
```

Prince Eric
Ariel
Flounder
King Triton
Max
Scuttle
Sebastian
Ursula

Eric and Ariel are collecting shells, stones and sticks on the beach. They've arranged them in two different patterns.

Can you finish each pattern by filling in the blank spaces with shells, stones or sticks?

Everyone in the kitchen wants to cheer Belle up with a show.
Find the matching dishes, cups, forks and knives.
Circle the ones that are the same.

There are 7 odd and silly things happening in this picture. Can you find them all? Here are some hints:

- What's Gaston wearing on his head?
- There's a fire somewhere.
- Someone is walking on his hands.
- What an odd-looking bicycle.

- Take a look at Gaston's feet.
- It looks like Belle is going swimming!
- An animal has escaped from the farm!

Be a reader like Belle!
Cut along the dotted lines to create two bookmarks.

Let's read a story together!

Reading can take you to far-off places!

© Disney

© Disney

Help Belle and the Beast build a snowman with eyes, arms, a nose and a mouth. Don't forget his hat and scarf!

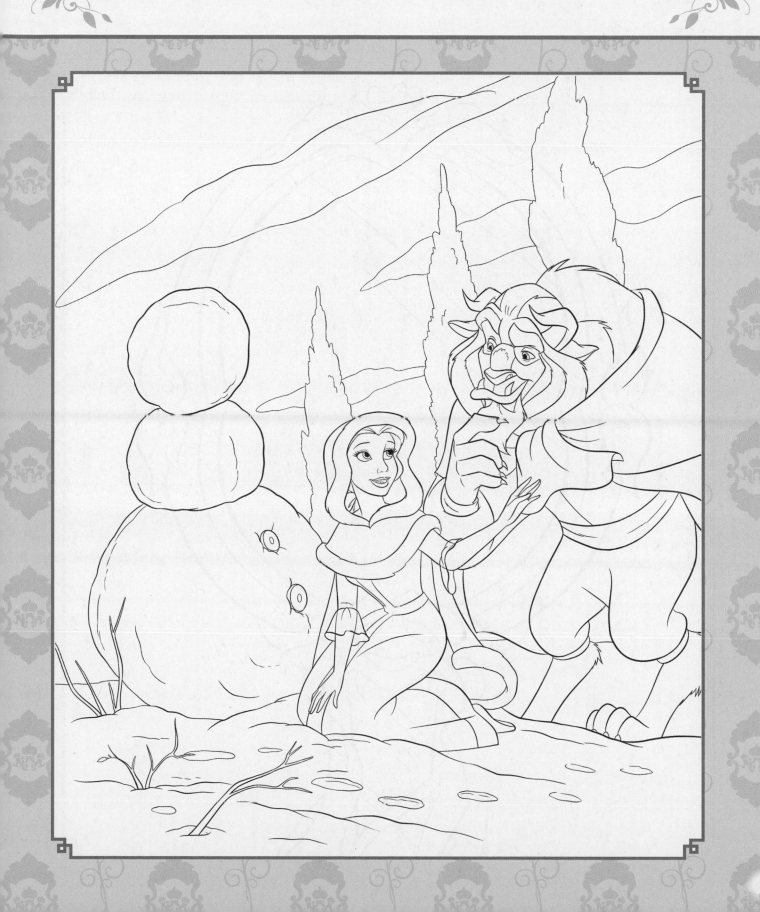

The Beast's Magic Mirror lets you see anyone you want.
Draw the person you would like to see in the Magic Mirror.

Write the names of the objects below in the crossword puzzle.

Across

1   4   6   7   8

Down

2   3   4   5

Can you find the following 10 objects hidden in the picture below?

- A glove
- A beach ball
- A cockerel
- A handbag
- A brush
- A cake
- A broom
- A pair of boots
- A comb
- A car

What kind of pet do Jasmine and Aladdin have?
Cross out all the 'u's and 'b's to find the answer to the riddle.

bau ufublubuyiunbg bucuabur-bupubuetb!

Jasmine and Aladdin are ready for a reading adventure!
Cut along the dotted lines to create two bookmarks.

Read a book
and discover
a whole new
world!

Every book
holds a new
adventure!

© Disney

© Disney

Jasmine wore the same outfit and accessories twice this week. Which two days did she wear the same things?

_____ and _____

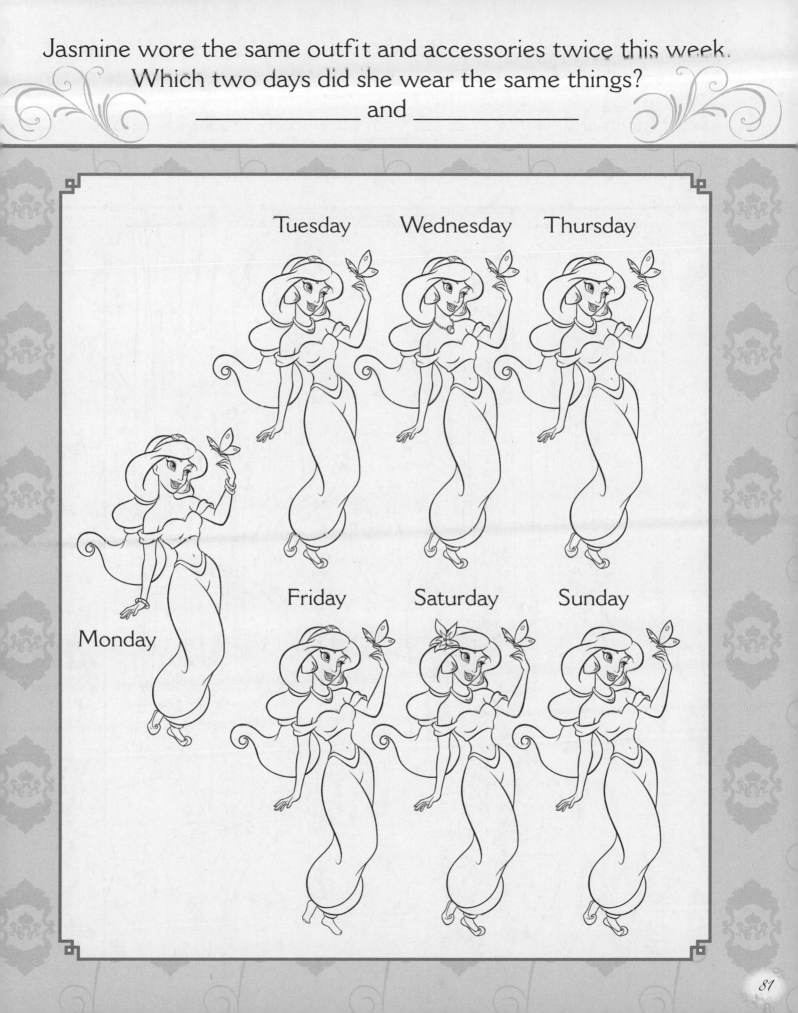

Look at this picture of Pocahontas, John Smith and their woodland friends. Then answer the questions below.

1. How many deer? _____   3. How many rabbits? _____

2. How many squirrels? _____   4. How many raccoons? _____

Help Pocahontas find her way through the forest to John Smith.

FINISH

START

How many butterflies do you see in the picture?
Write the number below.

I see _____ butterflies.

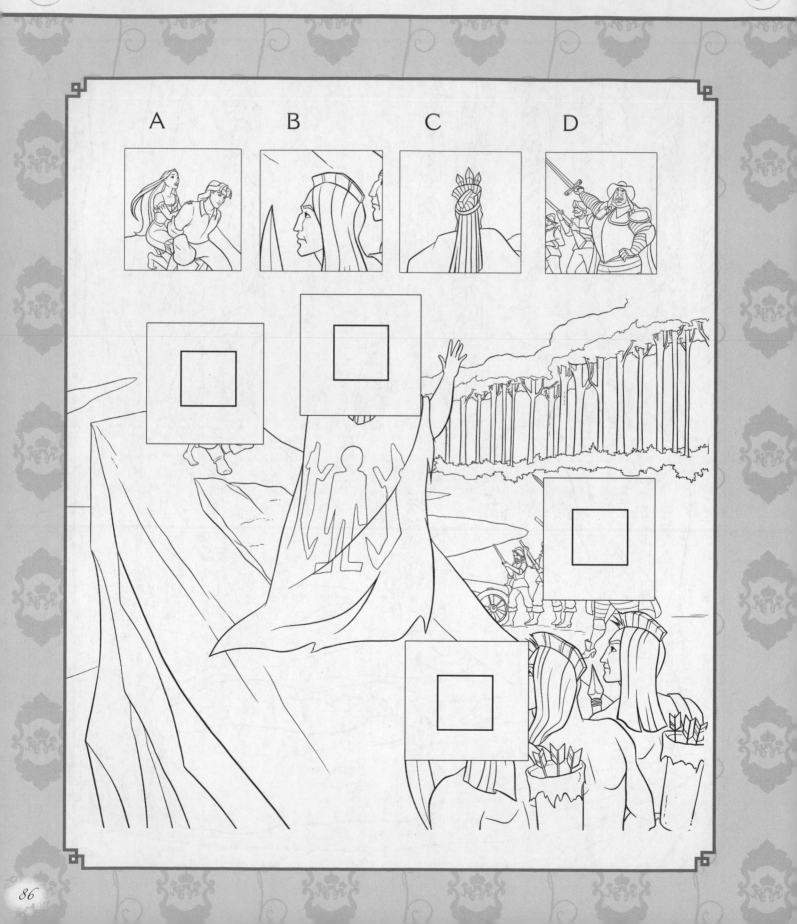

Write the names of the animals and objects below in the crossword puzzle.

Across

Down

Mulan needs to get to the Emperor. Can you help her?

START

FINISH

Help Shang train his men. Can you find six things that are different in the second picture?

Complete this scene with the small pictures below.
Write the letter of each picture in the correct white box.

A   B   C

Help the Matchmaker find the two Mulans who are the same.

Write the names of the people and things below in the crossword puzzle.

Across

3

5

7

Down

1

2

4

6

Each of the rows below must have four princesses:
Snow White, Aurora, Cinderella and Belle.
Fill each empty box with the correct letter.

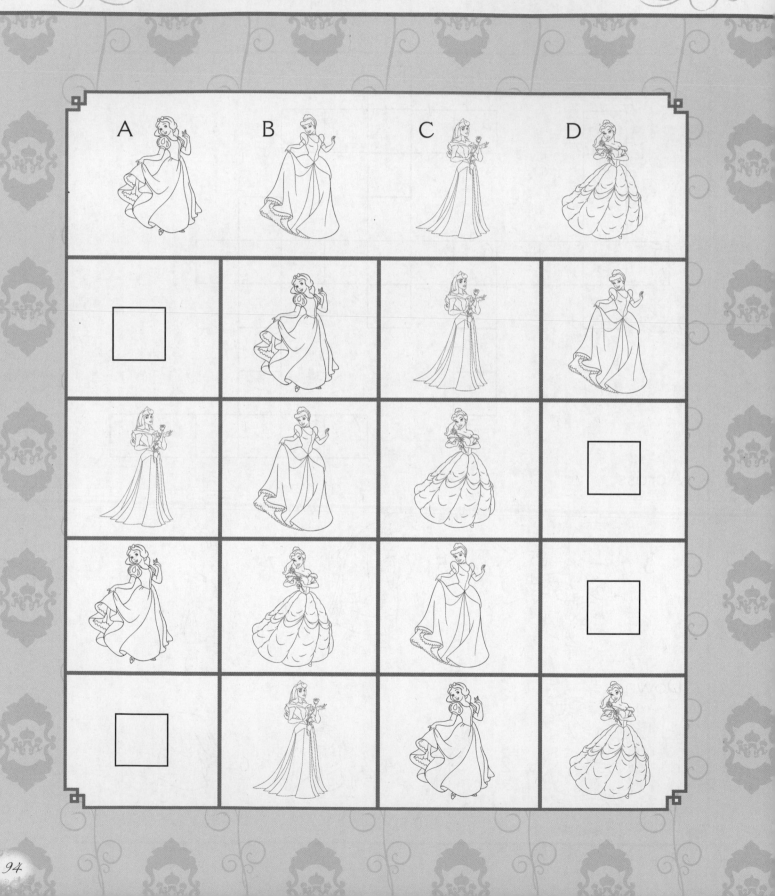

Ask an adult help you cut out each picture, punch a hole at the top and thread a ribbon through the hole. Then decorate your room with these beautiful princesses!

Draw a picture of yourself as a princess
on the back of the decorations.

© Disney

© Disney

© Disney

© Disney

96

Ask an adult to help you cut out each picture, punch a hole at the top and thread a ribbon through the hole. Then decorate your room with these beautiful princesses!

Draw a picture of yourself as a princess on the back of the decorations.

© Disney

© Disney

© Disney

© Disney

Draw a line from each princess to her shadow.

Answers

Page 52
1. Dopey, 2. Bashful,
3. Sneezy, 4. Sleepy,
5. Happy, 6. Grumpy,
7. Doc.

Page 53
1. 4 birds, 2. 5 butterflies,
3. 3 rabbits, 4. 2 squirrels,
5. 1 turtle.

Page 54
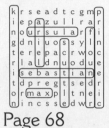

Page 56

Page 58

Page 60

Page 61
Flora gives the gift of BEAUTY.
Fauna gives the gift of SONG.

Page 62

Page 64

Page 66
1. 2 seagulls, 2. 3 frogs,
3. 4 fish, 4. 3 flamingos.

Page 67

Page 68

Page 69

Page 70

Page 75

Page 76

Page 77
A flying car-pet.

Page 81
Tuesday and Thursday.

Page 82
1. 3 deer, 2. 4 squirrels,
3. 2 rabbits, 4. 1 raccoon.

Page 83

Page 84
I see 22 butterflies

Page 85

Page 86

Page 87
C matches Pocahontas's canoe.

Page 88

Page 89

Page 90

Page 91

Page 92
7 and 9

Page 93

Page 94

Page 99

Disney PRINCESS

Beautiful Colouring

Use your favourite colouring pens or crayons to
make these princess pictures look magical.

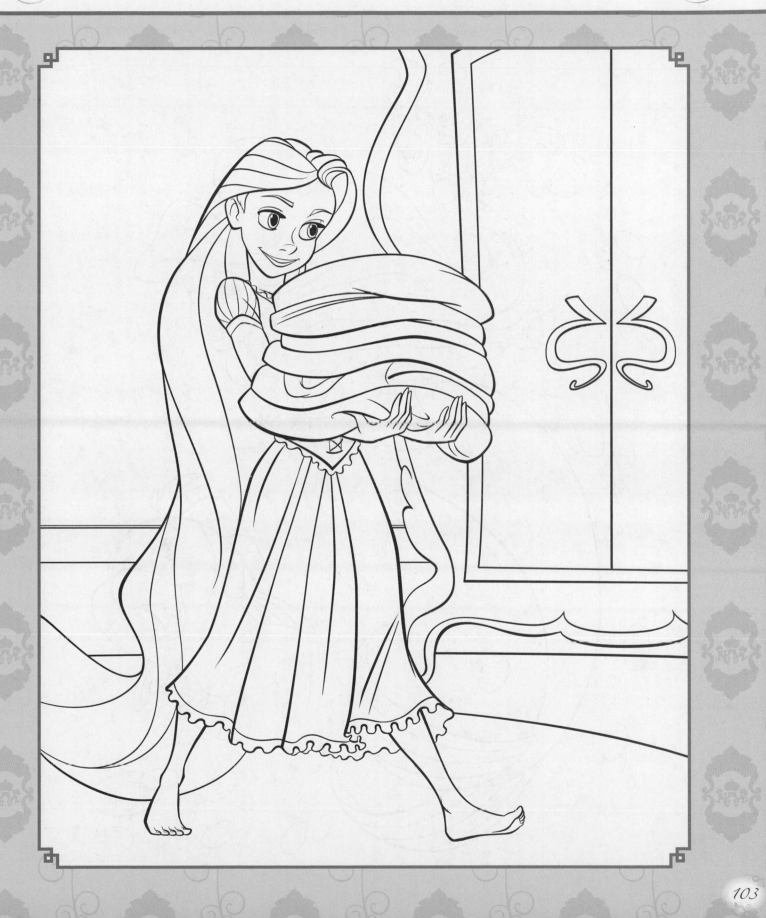

Ariel loves being a princess in a castle.

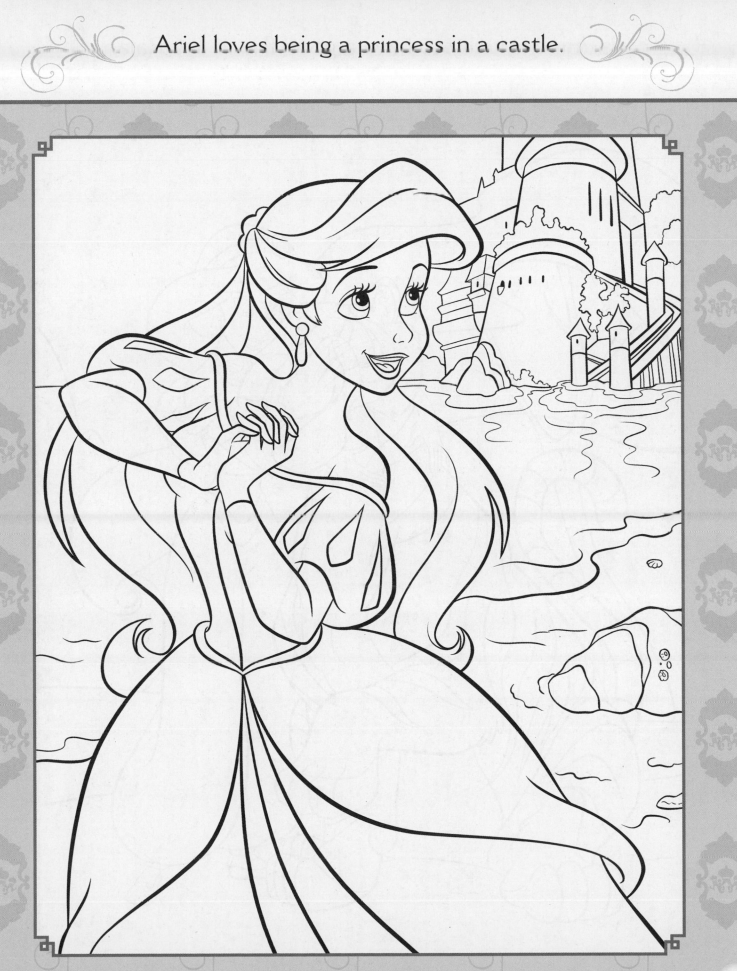

Jasmine is lucky to have a good friend like Rajah.

Belle reads to the children of the village.

Belle likes to ride with Phillip through the woods.

Merida hates it when her mum, Queen Elinor, brushes her hair.

Flounder cares for his friend Ariel very much.

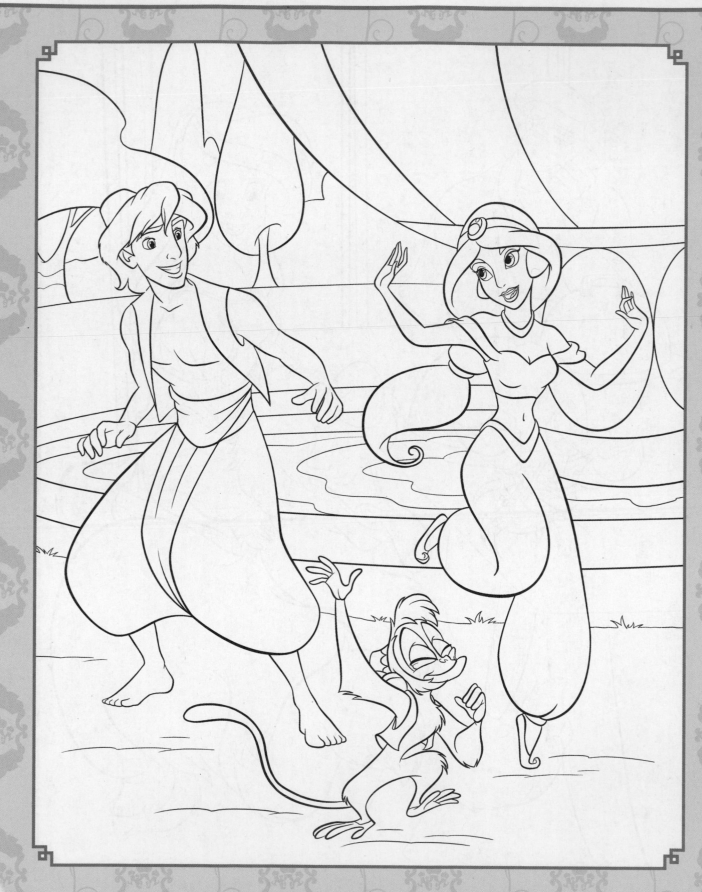

Aurora arrives home after a walk in the woods.

Aurora adds small sugar roses to a birthday cake.

Charlotte lends one of her fancy dresses to Tiana.

Tiana looks like a princess.

The Prince and Belle read their favourite book together.

Cinderella has made a special treat for Jaq's birthday.

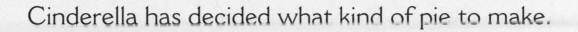
Cinderella has decided what kind of pie to make.

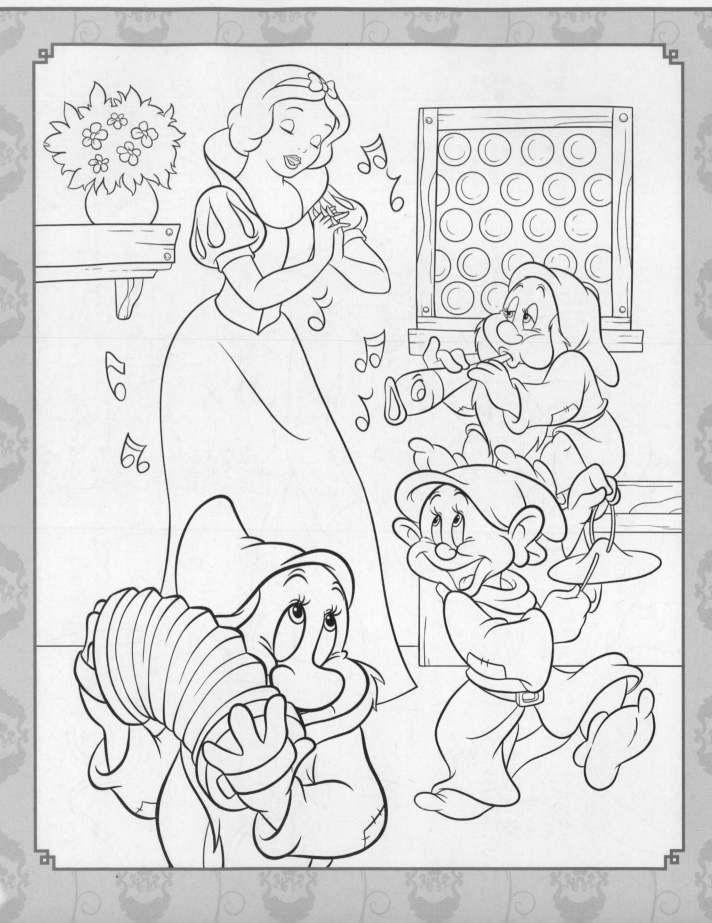

Snow White and the Prince take a walk in the meadow under the moonlight.

Rapunzel and Flynn share a quiet moment
on the lake as they wait for the floating lights.

Merida can't move in her formal dress!

"I'll be shooting for my own hand!"

"I'll be shooting for my own hand!"

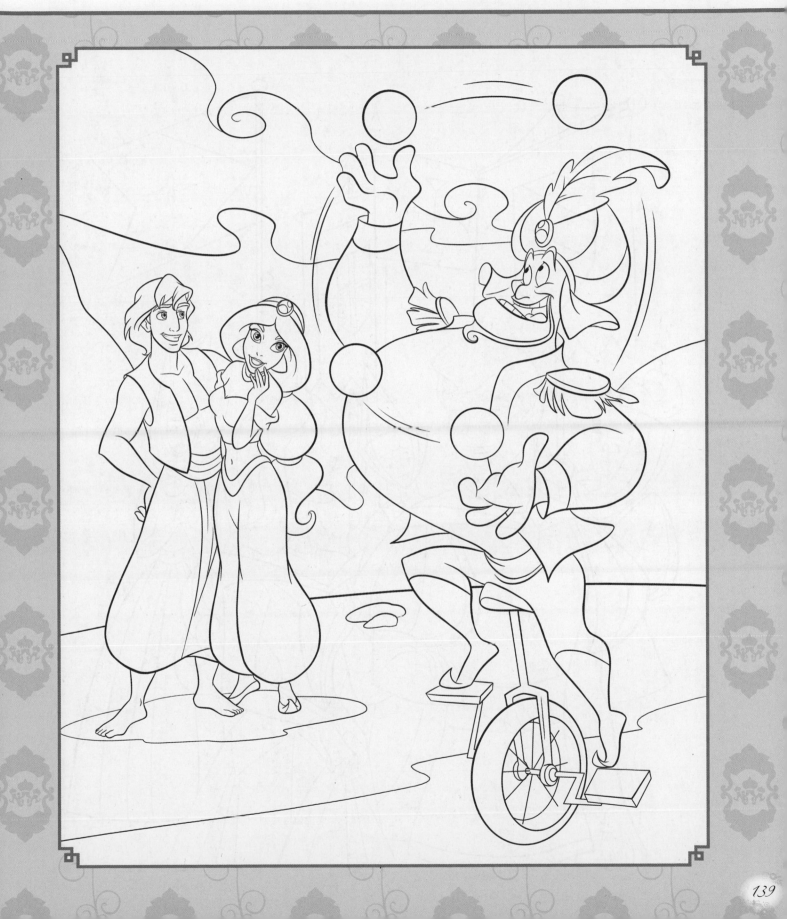

Everyone in the kingdom celebrates Aurora's birthday.

Let's get ready for a picnic!

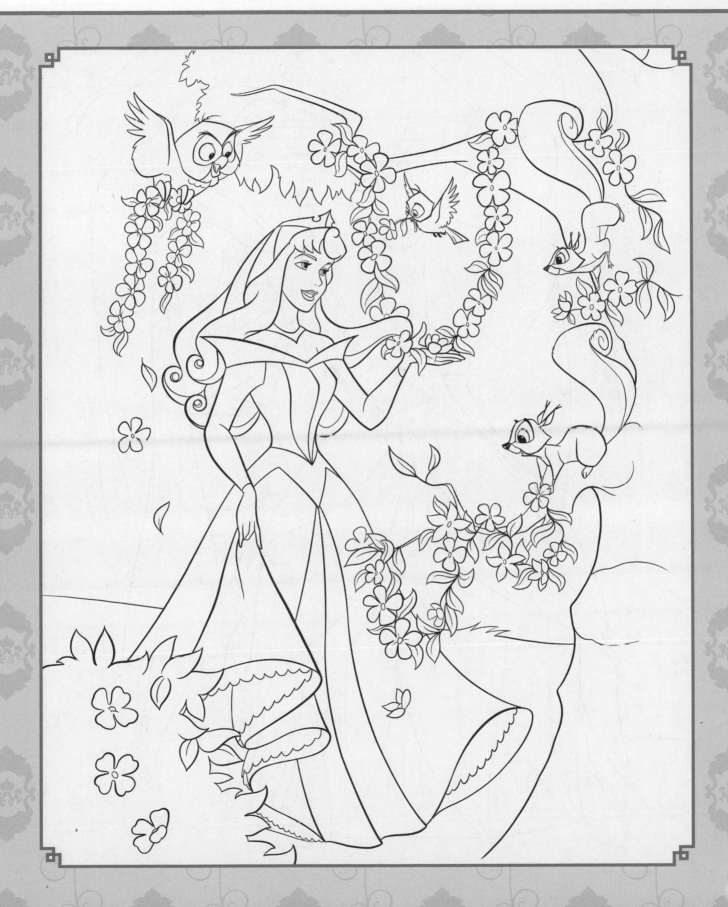

Tiana becomes a princess when she marries Prince Naveen.

Naveen and Tiana make a perfect couple.

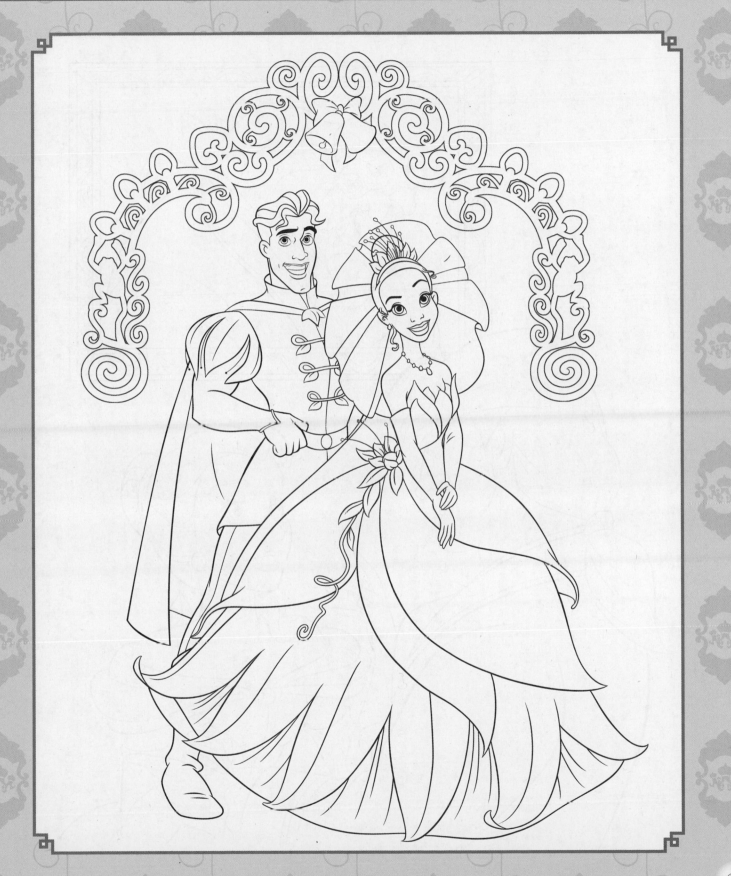

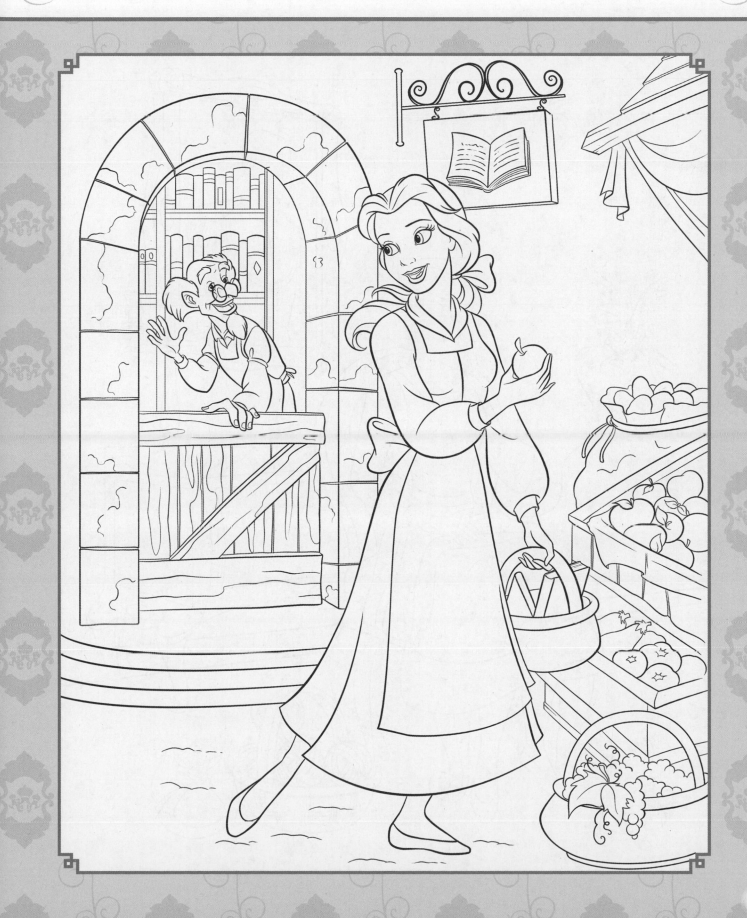

Cinderella's favourite vegetables are broccoli and tomatoes.

Snow White feeds her bird friends.

Rapunzel is filled with wonder as she looks
at the floating lights up close for the very first time.

Flynn and Rapunzel launch their own lantern into the sky.

Ariel will never forget her life under the sea.

Merida's favourite thing to do is ride with Angus through the forest.

Prince Phillip and Aurora go for
a ride through the countryside.

Tiana looks beautiful in the bayou!

Naveen and Tiana wave as they leave the church.

Cinderella remembers the ball
and how she lost one slipper.

Cinderella gives Major a treat.

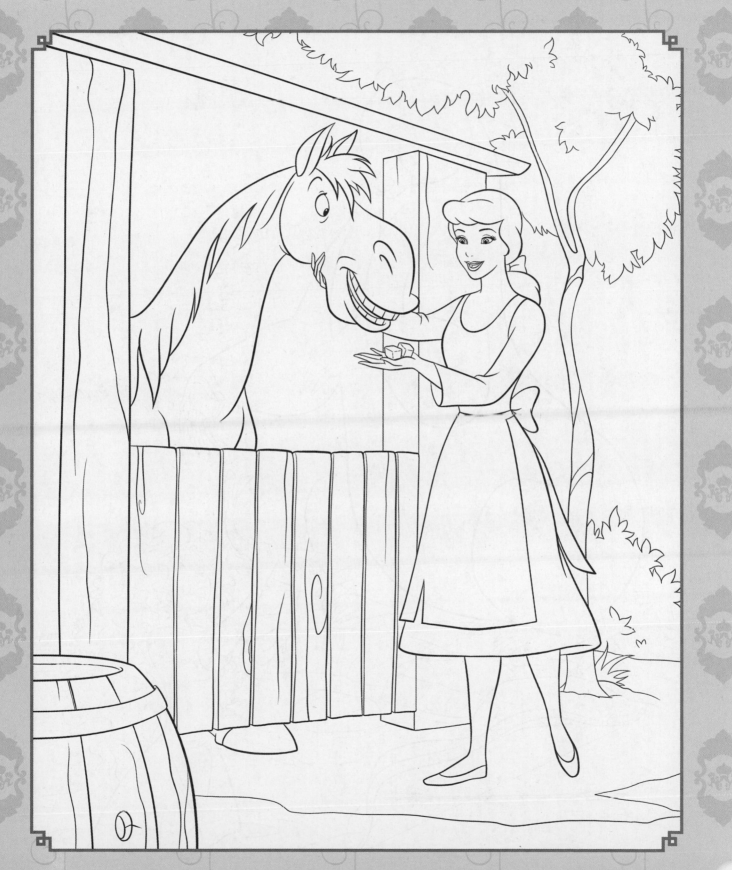

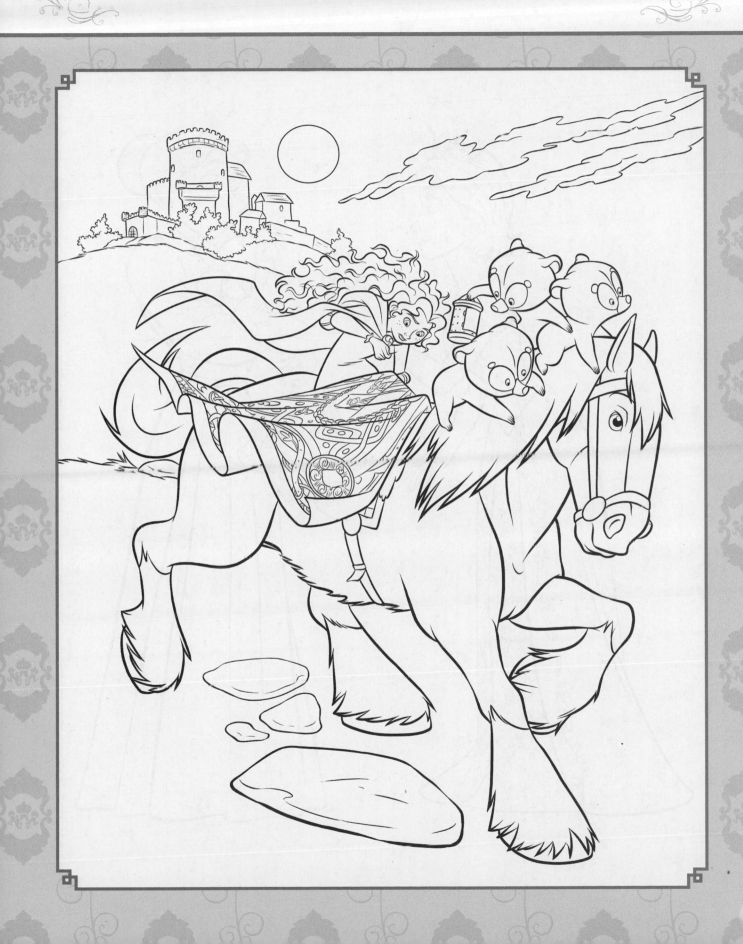

As a reformed thief, Flynn sheepishly returns the crown to its rightful owner.

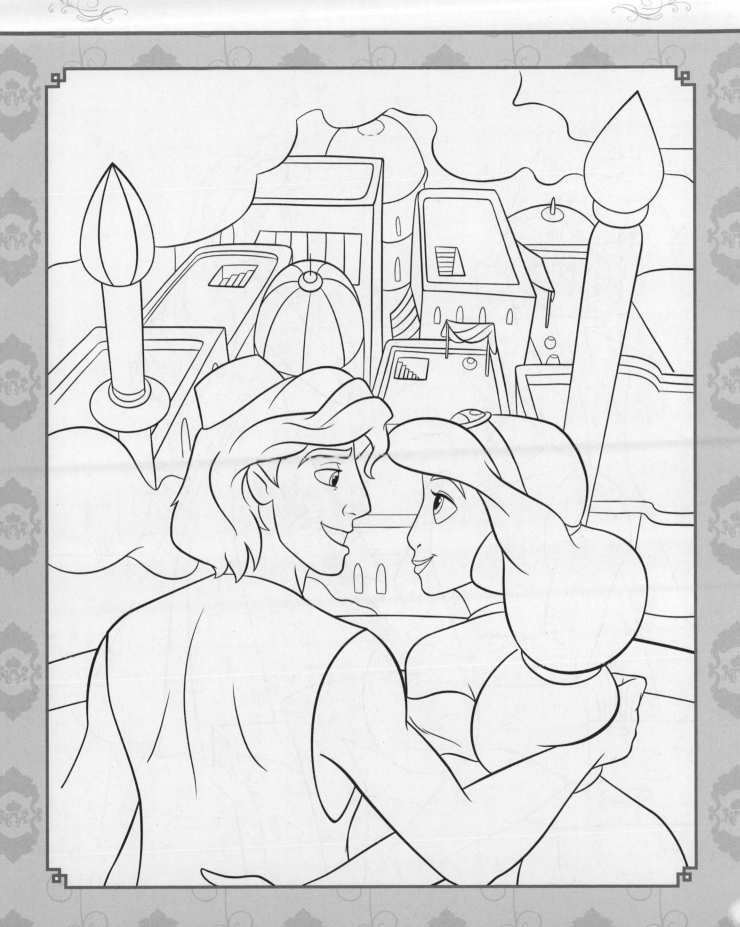

Aurora loves listening to music.

Prince Charming and Cinderella
take Bruno for a brisk walk

Belle and the Perfect Pearl

By Ellen D. Risco

Illustrations by the Disney Storybook Art Team

Belle threw open the doors. "I knew it. More beautiful adventures – tucked away and forgotten, maybe even unread!" she said.

It wasn't that the Beast didn't use the library. But when he did, he always read the same book.

"My library is your library," he liked to remind Belle. "Read and enjoy any book you find."

It hadn't been long since Belle had agreed to stay at the castle in return for her father's freedom. But each day she was getting to know the Beast better. She was starting to think that he actually cared about her happiness.

So Belle took the Beast at his word and made herself at home in the library. On many days, she spent hours there, reading book after book, losing all track of time.

Belle considered books priceless treasures. So when she took a break from reading, she gave the books special attention. Belle asked Featherduster to help her dust them.

She placed fallen books back on the shelves.

She pressed flat any folded pages.

One morning, Belle noticed the Beast had left his
favourite book lying open on the arm of his chair. "That's
not good for the binding," Belle said.

She picked up the book, closed it, then turned it over in her hands. Although the leather cover was worn, it was a beautiful volume with decorative gems on its brass clasp.

"Chip, look!" she said, pointing at the pearls. There was an empty hole where a fourth one should be.

Hmmm, thought Belle. *How long has it been missing?*

Belle looked around on the floor, in case it had fallen out just then.

Chip helped her search. "I found something!" he called. There by the library door was a single, perfect pearl.

"Let's see if it fits!" Belle suggested.

She dropped the pearl
into the hole in the clasp.
"Just right!" said Chip.

The Ugly Duck

But the pearl was loose and wouldn't stay put.

"I have an idea," Belle said. "This book is obviously your master's favourite. I'll fix it up a bit at a time. As the finishing touch, I'll reattach the pearl."

"Then you can surprise him!" Chip cried.

Belle nodded. She was happy to do something nice for the Beast.

Belle got right to work. She borrowed some rags and polish from Mrs Potts and gently cleaned the leather cover. Then she put the book back on the Beast's chair so he wouldn't miss it.

But when the Beast came into the library, he didn't pick up his book. He seemed to be looking for something.

"Can I help?" Belle asked.

"NO!" he bellowed. Then, more quietly, he added, "I mean, no. Excuse me." Without another word, he left the room.

Belle was startled but shrugged it off, assuming the Beast's bad mood would pass.

That afternoon, Belle did some
more work on the book. Carefully,
she smoothed out rumpled pages and
polished the brass clasp.

"I can see myself!" Chip said.

Again, Belle put the book back in its
place on the Beast's chair.

The Ugly
Duckling

Later that evening, Belle passed the Beast in the hall. She smiled and stopped to greet him. "Good evening –"

"Good night!" he snapped, hurrying by.

Belle stood there, a bit stunned. He hadn't even glanced her way.

Is something the matter? she wondered.

The next morning, it was time for Belle to add the pearl. But she wasn't sure she was ready to give the book to the Beast. He had been so grouchy the day before. *What will he be like today?* she wondered.

Just then, the Beast burst through the door. "You?" he cried. "You've had the pearl all along? I've been everywhere trying to find it!"

"Well, why didn't you say so!" Belle shouted, then she tossed the pearl on to the table. "By the way, I've been fixing up your book as a surprise."

The Beast was shocked.
He looked at the book. He picked
up the pearl. Then he smiled – and
began to laugh.

Belle stormed towards the door.

"Belle, wait," the Beast said. His gentle voice made Belle stop and turn. "I've been working on something for you, too."

In the Beast's hand was a lovely antique pin. "It's been in my family a long time," he explained. "I wanted you to have it. But first, I had something to add."

He placed the pearl on the pin, at the base of the rose. It fitted perfectly.

"I removed the pearl from my book yesterday," he said. "But I must have dropped it on my way out and –" He looked down. "I'm sorry I blamed you."

Now it was Belle's turn to laugh. "Well, I'm sorry I stole your surprise."

Belle pinned the gold rose with the perfect pearl to her dress. Then she watched as the Beast noticed his book's shining brass clasp, polished cover and smooth pages.

"Thank you, Belle," he said. "You've made it new."

Belle and the Beast still had much to learn about one another. But their hearts were in the right place.

Merida and the Missing Gem

By Lyra Spenser
Illustrated by IBOIX and Andrea Cagol

"Och!" Merida complained. "I spent all month working on a fancy brooch for Mum. But her birthday's tomorrow and it's still not right!"

Maudie clucked in sympathy, but didn't reply. As cook and nursemaid at Castle DunBroch, she was more worried about her latest batch of hot muffins.

"Mm! Who are those for?" asked Merida.

"Don't touch! These are for the DunBroch Brownie, the wee elf that lives outside the gate. He keeps things right in our castle," Maudie replied.

"Have you ever seen him?"

"Brownies don't like to be seen by humans," explained Maudie.

"But every day I leave him muffins, milk – and thistles for good luck. If the Brownie isn't happy, who knows what mischief he could make? Especially with the queen's birthday tomorrow."

Merida sighed again, thinking about her mum's birthday.

The brooch had started as a good idea. Merida chose a beautiful smoky quartz, her mother's favourite gem.

Then she designed the setting herself.

But when it was all put together, it didn't seem right.

Maybe, she thought, she should take another look at the gem....

But it was gone!

Then Merida saw
her brothers' guilty faces.
The wee devils must
have taken it!

Merida quickly realized what had happened.
Her brothers hadn't meant to cause trouble.
They'd only 'borrowed' the brooch because it
had looked so royal on their capes.

But somehow, as they played, the brooch had
become lost.

"Oh, come now lads!" said Merida. "You must
have dropped it somewhere. Think!"

Merida looked more closely at Hubert's shirt.

"Is this a thistle?" she asked. Then she looked at the others. "Are those crumbs on your shoes? Is that milk on your face?"

Suddenly, Merida had a very good idea where the triplets had been playing that morning.

Merida led the boys down near the gate, under the bridge, to a large, flat rock.

"Just as I thought," Merida said. "You ate the treats that Maudie made for the DunBroch Brownie!" She nodded. "So now we know where you lost the gem."

Merida and her brothers looked all around the clearing … but they couldn't find the brooch.

Merida had another thought. "What if the Brownie took the brooch because you three ate his treats? Maudie said he makes mischief if he isn't taken care of."

Quickly, she gave each of the boys different tasks.

Hamish got more muffins.

Hubert got more milk.

Harris got more thistles.

And Merida tidied up the clearing.

Merida set up the tray and rearranged the
thistle bouquet.

The boys looked at each other. They weren't
so sure about Brownies.

But Merida had no doubts. She told her brothers to hide and be still.

Nothing happened.

Then Merida remembered that Brownies
don't like humans to see them. So she tried
something else.

"DunBroch Brownie," Merida whispered into the air, "we're sorry your treats were taken! But we tried to fix everything. Could you help us, in return?"

There was only silence. Finally, they opened their eyes.
And then Harris spotted something shiny in the crook
of a tree – it was the brooch! Had the Brownie really just
returned it? Or had it been there the whole time?

And even stranger, when Merida examined the gem more closely, she saw that something was very different about it.

The next evening, Merida presented the birthday brooch to her mother.

"My favourite gem, set in a silver thistle!" Elinor exclaimed. "What better luck could I have than to have you as my daughter?"

Beaming, Merida knew that everything was set right, and things were positively ... perfect.